THE A[illegible]zing ADVENTURES OF Daring Daisy & THE WILDERNESS CREW

By
Andy Lucas

First published in 2018 by ALB

www.andylucasbooks.com

First Edition

for Daisy

I finally found time to write down some of those bedtime stories for you.

Dad x

CHAPTER 1

The Mysterious Box

Princess Daisy was bored, as she usually was every weekend.

She wasn't a real princess, of course, but her dad had been calling her that for as long as she could remember. Daisy preferred to think of herself as 'Daring Daisy', an explorer and adventurer. She just hadn't had any adventures yet!

Daisy lived with her parents, two hugely annoying older brothers called James and Max plus two gorgeous German Shepherd dogs named Smokie and Rysa.

They lived in a small town called Sunnyfield, just outside London.

Daisy was ten years old; bright, confident and full of curiosity about the world around her. She had long, dark hair and a pair of piercing blue eyes that shone with intelligence. Tall and slim, she was growing fast. At least that's what her parents regularly moaned to her about whenever they had to buy her new clothes.

Why were her weekends boring? Well, that was easy.

Firstly, her parents always focused on cleaning, washing and never ending decorating. The house always seemed to be in a mess no matter how much they cleaned or tidied.

As for her brothers, they just stayed in their bedrooms, glued to computer games. They were both much older than her so neither of them played with her.

Her dad was always covered in paint. All he did every Saturday and Sunday was drill things, hammer things and generally build things that were supposed to make their house look better.

Sometimes it worked and sometimes it didn't. Actually, Daisy was not convinced that he did anything other than make more mess that then needed cleaning up!

It was mid-morning, on a gloomy, rainy Saturday. Daisy was up in her bedroom, staring forlornly out of the window at the back garden. Up and dressed for hours, wearing her favourite blue jeans and bright green fleeced top, her plan to take herself off for a bike ride to the park was on hold while it was so wet.

It was early May. Their two oak trees and three apple trees already wore a coat of fresh green leaves. The long rectangle of lawn was lush and a little longer than it should have been but her dad hadn't got around to mowing it for the past few weeks.

It was a job on his list, she heard him keep telling her mum.

Still, as the rain grew noticeably heavier; hammering hard against the glass and running down the outside in playful rivulets, Daisy sighed to herself. It was definitely going to be another weekend of boredom, she decided.

A wasted weekend always felt like such a shame to her, especially because of how much she longed for each one to arrive when she was sitting in her classroom.

Often she would stare out of the window because the lessons were so tedious and her teacher; Miss Bramthwaite, always seemed to work with the other kids.

Daisy often found herself frustrated when she wasn't able to get help to answer a question or extend an answer but stupid old Bramthwaite always threw words at her like *resilience, independence* or *attitude* whenever she dared to complain.

Daisy loved writing but thought the curriculum was ridiculous. After all, she was *only* ten years old and she couldn't care less what a determiner was, or how to use the active voice. When she wanted to write a story, she just wanted to get on with it but this wasn't allowed anymore in school.

That was why Daisy had three large notebooks at home, already filled with exciting stories she'd written for herself. This way, she could write whatever she wanted without Bramthwaite's marking comments picking her up for not including adjectival phrases or adding enough subordinate clauses!

In a nutshell, this always left Daisy wishing for the weekends to arrive but then hating them when they failed to live up to expectations.

Feeling deflated, ignored, fed up and even a little bit sad, she resigned herself to another wasted Saturday.

Luckily, this time, she was in for a surprise. The doorbell rang downstairs. Once, twice.

Daisy half listened as she stared out at the oak tree and watched a couple of sparrows squabbling angrily over a juicy spider. She heard her mum speaking to someone, followed by the sound of the door closing.

'Daisy,' her mum called up the stairs. 'There's a parcel for you.'

A parcel for me? It wasn't her birthday for months. Who would be sending her anything?

Intrigued, Daisy dived downstairs. Her mum had already vanished back into the kitchen but she immediately spotted a decent-sized parcel, propped up by the front door.

Wrapped in old-fashioned brown paper and covered with dozens of strange-looking, brightly coloured stamps, she felt a warm flutter of excitement tickle at the base of her spine.

'Who can this be from?' she wondered aloud. 'We'll soon see,' she told herself, grasping the parcel quickly and hurrying back up the thickly carpeted stairs to her bedroom.

Shutting herself inside, Daisy sat on her neatly made bed and laid the parcel next to her.

'Let's see what you are.'

Usually, she was an expert at tearing open wrapping paper in seconds. At Christmas time, everyone marvelled at how fast she opened her gifts. Today, though, something inside told her to take some time.

Perhaps whatever was inside was fragile, or expensive?

As she started to pick at the many layers of sticky tape which sealed the paper joins, Daisy's eyes wandered over the stamps.

Not only were they bright and unfamiliar to her but the words printed on them were not even in English.

Some of them even seemed to be symbols rather than words, as though she was back in a maths lesson at school.

Shaking her head, she concentrated on the tape and soon had it coming off in long strips; pulling it free from the paper with some difficulty. Whoever wrapped it had clearly wanted to make sure it arrived in one piece.

In the end, it took five minutes of careful, painstaking work but eventually the final piece of tape was pulled off and her fingers started to peel apart the brown paper covering. As she worked, she noticed her hands were trembling a little and she caught herself holding her breath.

'How ridiculous,' she scolded herself firmly. 'Why are you getting so excited about a parcel wrapped in brown paper?'

Beneath the paper was a similarly drab cardboard box. Taking off the lid, Daisy stared down at yet another box nestled inside. This was not made of cardboard but rather from black metal. The sides were smooth but a series of strange etchings marked the top.

Daisy lifted it out and turned it over in her hands carefully. With no noticeable joins or seams, it appeared solid but it was far too light, as if hollow inside.

On the base, Daisy suddenly spotted a circular recess, no larger than her thumbnail. Inside the recess, a single red button stared back at her.

It reminded her of the story of Alice in Wonderland. Instead of a small bottle tempting her to drink, this tiny red button was silently urging her to press it.

'You get an unexpected parcel, with no note or message inside,' Daisy recapped to herself. 'Inside, you find a strange metal box with a single button. This is crazy.'

Daisy could just imagine her two brothers sniggering together just outside her bedroom door as they waited for her to press the button.

'It'll probably blow up with stinky smoke or something scary will jump out at me when I press it,' she huffed. 'I bet James and Max have done this. Brothers are *so* annoying!'

That was why she didn't press it. Fed up at the idea her brothers were playing a trick on her, she put the box on her dressing table and promptly forgot about it.

The rain didn't let up for another hour but eventually she was able to pull on her coat, fasten her cycle helmet, and head down to the park for a much-needed breath of fresh air.

The local park was huge and well tended. It had a narrow gravel path that ran all the way around its edge; passing through a small woodland and running alongside a graceful, giggling stream which was swollen by the rain. As she pedalled, Daisy passed dozens of grown ups, walking their dogs or jogging. She saw no other children.

Over three miles long, the path provided a lovely ride, ending at a large playground.

Daisy hoped to see some of her friends in the playground but the rain had kept them all away. The brightly coloured equipment was deserted; soaking wet and useless to play on.

Back home, after a dull lunch of jam sandwiches and a green apple, she found herself back in her bedroom, peering out of the window again. Darkening skies in the distance were lit up by occasional lightning flashes and accompanied, moments later, by grumbles of irritated thunder.

Surprisingly, Daisy did not take much notice of the approaching thunderstorm even though she was usually terrified of them. Her attention was strangely drawn back to her bed and the black metal box that now sat on it.

She knew she'd left it on her dressing table before heading to the park so why was it now on her bed? It had to be her stupid brothers again, she decided. Why couldn't they just leave her alone?

Then again, maybe it wasn't a horrible trick? What if they'd actually done something nice for once and she would find a lovely present inside?

To find out, she needed to press the button. After all, they couldn't do anything really bad to her because they'd get into trouble.

Daisy's thoughts were momentarily interrupted by a warm, wet nose being thrust into one hand, followed by a sticky lick on the other.

Looking down, she smiled softly at the two frightened dogs who were now sitting on either side of her; both staring up through intelligent brown eyes that pleaded with her to protect them from the noise monster.

Smokie and Rysa were fully grown and beautiful. Long coated, black and tan, they were both very soppy despite looking fierce. Whenever a storm hit, they normally huddled together beneath the stairs, cowering and whimpering.

'Oh, my heroes,' Daisy laughed, ruffling them behind their ears before having to fend them off as they jumped up excitedly for more fuss. Both dogs were taller than her when they stood up on their hind legs so having them jumping up at her for attention and protection was a little too much.

Still giggling, she playfully pushed them away.

'No, boys. Down! Be good. The storm won't hurt you. Get up on the bed. You can stay here with me.'

Needing no further encouragement, the dogs bounded up onto the bed and spun happily around on the spot as they picked out the best place to flop down. Smokie's excitedly wagging tail smacked into the metal box, sending it flying.

'It's going to get broken soon, whatever it is,' she told them. 'Might as well get this over with.'

Kneeling down on the carpet, she picked the box up and sucked in a breath. The button was already facing upwards where the box had overturned in flight.

Wasting no more time, she pressed the button firmly. When nothing happened, she tried again, pressing as hard as she could. There was no click or buzz. Nothing. What an anti-climax. The stupid thing didn't even work!

Angrily, Daisy shoved the box away and climbed onto her bed with the dogs, twisting around to find a space for herself. Then she turned on the television and lost herself in a couple of music videos.

When the storm hit fully, it literally shook the house with the force of a dozen thunderclaps and she was secretly glad the dogs were with her. The three of them rode out the storm together, warm and safe in her bedroom.

It wasn't until the middle of the night that Daisy gave the box another thought.

Woken suddenly, a little after one o'clock, it had begun to hum and vibrate like a mobile phone ringing on silent mode. Persistent and demanding, it clamoured for her attention.

Rubbing the sleep from her eyes, she slid out from beneath her covers and sat on the floor. Alone in the room now, the dogs had long since gone back downstairs after the storm passed.

In the dim light cast by her fairy princess night light, plugged in by the door, Daisy noticed the box had changed. A new recess had appeared next to the small one housing the red button. More importantly, she could see there was something inside it.

Reaching in carefully, her fingertips closed around a slip of paper. Pulling it out, she shuffled closer to her night light to study it.

A brief sentence stared up at her from the paper, in printed type.

Take me outside.

Daisy looked towards the window. The curtains were open and she could see a clear night sky, brightly lit by a full moon. No rain, she thought. That was good. Yet going outside, alone, in the middle of the night seemed scary?

She wondered whether she should wake her parents and tell them about the strange box but something deep inside seemed to be saying that everything would be okay.

In the end, she decided to do as the message asked.

Dressing quickly in jeans and her thickest jumper, she pulled on her coat. Carrying the box carefully down the stairs, she padded into the kitchen which was at the rear of the house. Unlocking the back door, she summoned her courage, turned the handle quietly and slipped out into the darkness.

The air was calm and surprisingly mild for such a late hour. Stars shone brightly above her head, adding a billion twinkles to the dazzling moonlight.

Stepping cautiously away from the back door a few paces, she set the box down on the long, wet grass and waited.

Now what? She didn't know what she was waiting for. She'd pressed the red button several times already but did she need to press it again? Why hadn't it come with instructions?!

As it turned out, Daisy didn't have to wait very long. While she was deciding what to do next, the top of the box silently began to shimmer and dissolve.

Open mouthed, she watched as a swirling cloud of purple smoke began to pour from inside the box and rise up into the night sky. As it got higher, it quickly expanded until a gigantic cloud hovered above the entire garden.

'My brothers couldn't do this,' she realised.

Eyes shining in amazement but hands clenched tightly together with uncertainty, she watched the cloud slowly begin to form into a solid shape.

Within a few seconds, a gigantic airship floated effortlessly above her and the cloud vanished. Sparkling with a ghostly silver light, the airship was more cylindrical than spherical. It actually looked a lot like one of the rugby balls that the teams kicked around in the games her dad loved to watch on television. Massive, she was sure it was over one hundred metres long.

Hanging below the huge balloon sat an impressive cabin, stretching for over thirty metres in length. It had three storeys when she counted the layers of windows.

A single door seemed to be the only way in or out. The cabin and balloon were joined together in one unit rather than a hot air balloon, where the basket hung below the balloon on ropes.

Daisy recognised what it was immediately from old pictures she'd seen on the internet, at school. Her class had recently finished a project on WWII and it looked very similar to airships that had hunted enemy submarines off the British coast.

She was just beginning to wonder if the surprises were over for the night when the airship cabin door slid open, high above her head. There was no sound at all as she watched a long rope ladder snake down until the end touched the grass by her feet.

It was all so bizarre that she found herself laughing. 'I may as well see what happens next.' She felt much braver now that she knew she *must* be dreaming.

Daisy was a brilliant climber. On the last school residential trip, she'd easily climbed ropes and poles that went almost as high as this. Hand over hand, foot after foot, she climbed determinedly up the rope ladder, which strangely did not move or sway in the way she expected. Up and up she went, soon reaching the doorway and pulling herself inside.

Standing up and brushing some imaginary dust from her coat, she should have been amazed at her surroundings but this was, of course, a dream so she simply accepted everything she saw.

At the front there was a large bank of computers, alive with images, numbers and maps. A pilot's chair was bolted in front of it.

Towards the rear sat a large lounge area, complete with three gigantic sofas in brilliant shades of red, blue and yellow. Next to the lounge was an impressive kitchen, containing a gigantic, gold-coloured refrigerator.

Keen to explore before she woke up and the dream went away, Daisy hurried up a nearby set of stairs to the next floor where she discovered two large bedrooms, a bathroom and a games room, complete with a pool table, large screen television, computer gaming console and even a dart board! Daisy loved to play darts.

Finally, another flight of steps led her up to the top floor which was open, forming a single room. Even though she was dreaming, her heart lurched with excitement when she saw the beautiful swimming pool and bubbling hot tub.

Five minutes later, she was back down on the ground floor, examining the airship's controls. Sitting gingerly in the pilot's chair, she wondered if she should press one of the many buttons or perhaps pull one of the small switches.

'What do I do now?' she asked herself quietly.

Unexpectedly, a soft, female voice answered her immediately, coming from the computer console directly in front of her.

'Good evening,' said the voice. 'I am Val, your flight control computer. How can I help you, Miss Daisy?'

'Er...how do you know my name, Val?' Daisy asked uncertainly. 'Where am I?'

'That's easy,' replied Val cheerfully. 'This is your airship and you are now its pilot. This airship will take you wherever you wish to go.'

'I don't understand.'

'Of course you do,' disagreed Val politely. 'You've often wished to have amazing adventures. Now, you can.'

'How could you possibly know what I wish for? It's impossible.'

'You have always believed in magic, haven't you?'

'Yes.' Daisy nodded, a smile forming on her lips without her even realising.

'This is the magic you've always wished for. Now it's up to you to use it wisely. To do good deeds.'

'To help people?' wondered Daisy, nodding.

'Exactly. Where do you wish to go, Miss Daisy?'

'Just call me Daisy, Val.'

'As you wish, Daisy. So, where to?'

Daisy pondered the question for a second before suddenly being overcome by a massive yawn that seemed to go on forever. Out of nowhere, she began to feel very sleepy.

'I don't have anywhere I want to go,' she sighed, stretching.

'Perhaps you should go back to bed then? There's plenty of time for adventures in the future,' suggested Val kindly. 'I'll be here whenever you need me.'

'I know this is a dream but it feels so real.'

'It isn't a dream,' Val promised. 'Would you like a snack before you go?'

'No thanks, Val.' Then Daisy was struck by a question. 'What kind of snack?'

'Anything you wish,' promised Val. 'The refrigerator in the kitchen is as magical as the rest of this airship. If you are every hungry, all you need to do is think very hard about what you want to eat, or drink,' Val added.

'Then what?'

'Then simply open the refrigerator door and it will be waiting for you.'

Daisy was very tempted to try it out but she was feeling very weary now.

'I'll look forward to wishing up some wonderful food another time.'

Too tired to carry on with such an exciting dream, she said goodbye to Val before making her way back down the rope ladder. Jumping off the last couple of rungs, she landed softly in the wet grass.

Immediately, the ladder started to pull itself up again, disappearing inside the cabin doorway. Then the door slid closed.

Daisy knew what she had to do next without really understanding *how* she knew. Reaching down, she pressed the red button on the box.

Above her head, the airship began to dissolve back into the swirling purple cloud again. Moments later, the entire airship was gone. The cloud formed a narrow funnel that emptied itself completely inside the magic box.

When every last wisp of cloud had been swallowed inside, the lid appeared out of thin air, sealing it shut.

Ready to fall asleep on her feet, Daisy scooped it up and headed indoors. Back up in her room, she placed the box carefully on the floor next to her bed, climbed beneath the cover and promptly fell fast asleep.

In the morning, Daisy awoke to the sound of rain drumming loudly on her window. Normally, the sound of more rain would have made her feel sad but not today.

Leaping out of bed, she felt a sense of excitement as she picked up the box from where she'd left it. Although she'd been dreaming, it had all *seemed* so real that she felt as if she'd actually had her first adventure.

She was turning the box over in her hands when a piece of paper fluttered out from somewhere inside and landed in her lap.

'That old message,' she told herself. But this message was different from the first one. Heart thumping, Daisy read it carefully. Twice.

Whenever you need to fly, press the button. Val.

Staring out at the pouring rain, Daisy smiled. As her mum called her down for breakfast, she pulled on her dressing gown and headed for the door, pausing to place the box on her dressing table.

It hadn't been a dream after all. It was real!

Val was real and the airship was real. The mysterious box was magical and, for some reason, it had chosen her. All she needed now was to find somebody to help.

Her humdrum life already seemed to be a thing of the past. The future called to her, offering exciting adventures that even *she* could not have dreamed of.

Daring Daisy to the rescue!

CHAPTER 2

Flood

The rain should have stopped by now. All the weather forecasts had said that the wet weather would be over by Wednesday but they couldn't have been more wrong.

Instead of having to wait for the weekend to have her next adventure with Val, Daisy was at home by

Tuesday lunchtime, when the Headteacher decided to close the school because of violent storms that were battering the country, one after another.

Local news reports focused on how a nearby river was getting too full to cope with so much water falling from the sky so quickly. They said it could burst its banks and the town would be flooded!

As her parents hurried around, getting extra supplies of food and bottled water from the shops before they closed, Daisy was left indoors with her brothers. Both of them seemed very excited by the prospect of a flood but her dad had told them both off.

'Floods are no joke,' he'd told them the night before. 'They're very dangerous. We need to be ready to leave if the police decide to evacuate the town.'

Despite the serious mood that filled their house on that day, Daisy had an ace up her sleeve. If the flood did strike, she would be ready. Not just to help her own family but to make sure she was ready to help anyone else who needed rescuing.

What she knew, but nobody else did, was that she now had a very special box. It had arrived in the post but she still had no idea who'd sent it, or why.

The magic inside it was very powerful. In her heart, she'd often dreamed of leading a life of adventure and excitement. Her vivid imagination would often whisk her away to distant lands where she would battle dragons, discover buried treasure and generally save the day.

The only problem with the box was that she'd moved it out of her bedroom the day before.

It was such an unusual box, she worried that her parents, or her brothers, might suddenly notice it. They might even take it away, especially as nobody knew who had sent it to her.

Deciding that she wanted it tucked away somewhere safe, Daisy had hidden it beneath some old seed packets at the back of their little garden shed. Nobody would go in there until summer time, she knew, so it had seemed the perfect hiding place, for the time being.

With the threat of a flood coming, she now seriously regretted her choice.

And still the rain fell, growing heavier all the time, leaving everyone wondering how the clouds could hold so much water.

As her family were all watching one of the weather updates, at a little after four in the afternoon, they received the news everyone had been dreading.

The river had begun to overflow. An evacuation had been ordered and residents needed to be ready to leave when the emergency services arrived at their door.

Her family were already prepared to go but their town, though small, still had thousands of people living in it. Daisy knew it might take some time before anyone came to get them.

Glancing out of the lounge window, which looked out onto the street, she noticed the drains were bubbling up and the rainwater had nowhere to go anymore. Water quickly started to overflow onto the pavement and then it began pouring into all the front gardens along her road.

'Come on,' said Dad quickly. 'The river water will reach us here soon too and then the flooding will get very bad, very fast.'

'Upstairs everyone,' commanded Mum, looking a little anxious but forcing a smile for the sake of the children. 'We can't stop the water getting inside the house but we'll all be safe upstairs until the rescue services get here.'

Any ordinary child would have been very happy to follow such sensible advice but Daisy was no ordinary girl.

When the water rose higher, the emergency services would do their best, she knew, but would they reach everyone in time?

As darkness closed in, the water level continued to rise until it poured in beneath their front door and quickly flooded the ground floor. Dirty, brown and stinking, it lapped hungrily at the bottom of the stairs, eager to swallow up more of their home. The electricity was off so they huddled together on the landing with a couple of torches and some scented candles for light.

It was time for Daring Daisy to act!

Pretending to be tired, she stifled a yawn and slipped off into her bedroom, carrying one of the torches with her. Her parents were going to stay awake, on the landing, to monitor the rising water and they were both quite pleased when their daughter seemed to want to go to bed. Sleep would be the best thing for her and at least she wouldn't be too scared by the unfolding disaster. They would wake her up when help came.

Little did they know that Daisy only remained in her bedroom long enough to slip on her coat and change into a pair of boots.

Sliding open her bedroom window carefully, she was immediately buffeted by a strong wind and soaked by driving rain. Shrugging it off, she hooked one leg over the sill and climbed out onto the window ledge.

The water's surface sat just over a metre below her window. The garden shed was her target but it was almost completely underwater. Only the very top of its apex roof poked above the swirling water, like a tiny island in a furious sea.

Scanning the water all around with her torch beam, she finally spotted exactly what she was looking for.

The swimming pool inflatables usually sat behind the shed. Her mum hadn't bothered deflating them last summer so two lilos and a giant doughnut were now bobbing merrily around her garden, kept from floating completely away by the tops of the garden fences, which were still just above water.

The doughnut was closest to the house; only a short distance away from her window. Another quick rummage in her room turned up a ball of string, which she swiftly tied around the leg of one of her large dolls.

Using it as a lasso, Daisy threw the doll towards the inflatable time and time again until, a few minutes later, the doll finally dropped through the hole in its centre.

Careful not to tug too hard, she held her breath as she slowly eased the ring back towards her; the doll's arms and legs jamming underneath nicely and acting as the perfect fishing hook.

Two minutes after reeling the doughnut in, Daisy was seated on top of it, using her hands to paddle determinedly towards the shed. The water felt cold but she ignored the discomfort. Reaching the roof quickly, she grasped it tightly.

The roof of the shed had needed replacing for years. It was fairly rotten and she had no problem pulling up one corner until the tired wood broke off in her hands, leaving a decent-sized hole.

'We can always blame the flood,' she muttered, bracing herself for what she needed to do next.

Daisy had been on the school swimming team for two years and had already earned three lifesaving badges. Swimming around inside a small shed would be easier than diving twelve feet down to the bottom of a pool to retrieve a large rubber brick, she told herself, although the dark water felt ominous and dangerous, cautioning her to reconsider.

In the end, to her relief, she didn't need to go diving after all. A few moments after opening the hole in the roof, there was a gurgling sound from inside and a small fountain of floating objects started popping up like an underwater volcano suddenly erupting.

The first few objects were useless; plastic flower pots and polystyrene garden kneelers. Then, to her relief, the box rose to the surface. Scooping it up, she paddled clear.

Wasting no time, Daisy pressed the secret button and sat back to watch the magic; still overawed to see her gigantic airship materialise from the cloud of purple smoke. Like before, the rope ladder snaked down towards her and she quickly scampered up, leaving the doughnut to float away down the garden.

Shutting the door against the wind and rain, Daisy felt a burst of optimism. Settling down into the pilot's seat, she took a deep breath.

'It is good to see you again, Daisy,' came a familiar voice. It was Val.

'Hi Val,' replied Daisy. 'There's been awful flooding. My parents said that people are stranded all over the place. The emergency services can't get to them all quickly enough. I think we should help.'

'That is why the magic was given to you,' Val agreed.

'Who actually sent the box to me anyway?' Daisy suddenly remembered to ask. It had been bugging her since it had first arrived.'

'That's not for me to say,' answered Val solemnly. 'Anything else, but not that.'

'Really?'

Daisy was about to argue but realised that now wasn't the time. There were people who needed her help.

'I have scanned all the news channels and the internet traffic to find where people might be trapped,' Val explained helpfully. 'At least twenty families have been cut off. The fire service has to get them out one at a time. The rain is forecast to continue so the water will carry on rising,' Val added.

'There's no time to lose,' decided Daisy firmly. 'Set a course for the families who are furthest away and who won't be rescued in time. They will be very scared, especially if they have very young children.'

'You're right, Daisy.'

The huge airship sprang to life as its gigantic, twin propellers began to spin. Slowly it rose up into the stormy sky. Shrugging off the battering wind and hammering rain as easily as an elephant ignores a buzzing fly, the airship turned in mid air and set off northwards, gaining altitude steadily.

In her chair, all Daisy actually had to do was sit and wait. Val was doing all the flying which gave her time to prepare herself for the rescuing that lay ahead.

'How long until we reach the first family, Val?'

'Five minutes,' replied Val. 'I'm taking us well away from the town so we don't bump into any other rescue aircraft. I know the police, ambulance and coast guard will all have sent their helicopters into the area.'

'Good idea, thanks,' agreed Daisy. 'Time to get ready.'

She spent those final minutes getting out a supply of blankets and towels, piling them up on the floor near the door. She also found a well-stocked medical kit just as the engines slowed and she felt the airship begin to sink.

'Lights, Val,' Daisy commanded and Val switched on a bank of exterior floodlights. Their broad beams shone downwards beneath the airship, lighting up a sorry sight indeed.

The house below the airship was flooded right up to its tiled roof and completely surrounded by angry water. It must be near the river, Daisy decided, when she noticed the strong currents swirling all around the house.

Anyone falling in would be swept away and even a strong swimmer wouldn't stand a chance.

Daisy suddenly caught her breath when she spotted a small huddle of people on the roof itself, hanging onto the chimney for all they were worth. Five pairs of frightened eyes stared up at her.

The three adults and two children had been waiting patiently to be rescued for over an hour. Despite wearing coats and hats, all of them were soaked to the skin and shivering.

Opening the door, Daisy watched as the rope ladder slowly lowered itself down until it touched the top of the chimney pot, within a metre of the stranded family.

She could see that two of the grown ups would be fine to climb up but the other one was an elderly woman who looked frail and exhausted. The two children were also very young; maybe three or four years old. They would need help too.

'Val, I need a harness like the fire service use.' Daisy couldn't help thinking of the episodes of Fireman Sam she used to watch, where Sam, Penny and Elvis always seemed to use a double harness to rescue people with the helicopter. 'Do we have one?'

'Of course,' said Val. Directing her over to a nearby storage cupboard, a double harness was soon hooked over Daisy's shoulder and she was gone, dropping down the ladder without a backwards glance.

Ignoring the icy wind and freezing rain that immediately stung her face, she was soon standing on the slippery roof and the rescue could begin.

The parents of the children looked amazed. They'd been expecting to see a fire fighter or a police officer, not a young girl.

'There's no time to explain,' Daisy said kindly. 'Come on. Let's get you all off this roof and to somewhere safe.'

'My children can't climb a ladder like this,' protested the younger woman, through chattering teeth.

'They don't have to.'

Daisy pulled off the double harness and quickly attached it to the bottom rung of the ladder, where it snapped securely into place.

'Is it safe?'

'Completely. It takes two at a time. One of you will need to go up with a child. The ladder will then come back down for the next. Who's first?'

'You go first, with Sally,' said her husband, giving her a reassuring hug.

Being brave but clearly scared, Sally looked to be nearer two years old now that Daisy could see her clearly.

'I'm not scared, Daddy. I'll look after Mummy,' she said firmly.

Slipping a harness over both of them was all that Daisy needed to do. The magic ladder knew what it had to do next and slowly pulled them up to the waiting airship; lifting them slowly and smoothly so Sally would not be too worried.

Actually, although Daisy could not see from below, the little girl's face was beaming with excitement as she was hauled upwards. What an adventure she was having!

Once safely aboard, the ladder returned to the rooftop. The man chose to stay and sent the boy and the old lady up next.

Five minutes later, everyone was safely inside the airship, out of the wind and rain.

Brushing off their questions, Daisy hurried around, offering blankets and checking that everyone was alright. Leaving the family to hug each other with relief, she pulled mugs of hot tea straight from inside the magic fridge, together with plates of delicious sandwiches, sticky chocolate fudge cake and fresh fruit.

After ten minutes, the grateful family allowed themselves to be moved into one of the upstairs bedrooms so that Daisy and Val could get back to work.

Six hours later, with twenty-three people aboard, all safe and sound, Val informed Daisy that everyone had been rescued. As daylight started to tickle the dark horizon, the huge airship made its way slowly to a nearby carpark which was perched high up on a nearby hill. Completely safe from the flood, it was already being used by the emergency services as a staging area.

Hundreds of people were there, being cared for by doctors and nurses, inside dozens of hastily erected tents.

'I'm afraid I can't stick around,' Daisy explained to her passengers.'

'We understand,' said Sally, stepping forward and giving her a hug. 'You're like a real superhero who needs to be secret.' The toddler beamed and tried a knowing wink which just ended up being a blink.

'Something like that,' chuckled Daisy. 'Now, let's get you all off.'

Descending until the airship hovered a few centimetres off the grass, she opened the door and hurried everyone outside, making sure to close the door quickly behind them.

Before any of the astonished police officers could head over towards them, Daisy shouted for Val to take off, which the computer happily did.

Leaving the stunned adults to watch helplessly from below, the gigantic airship lifted off again and was soon lost from sight in the stormy clouds.

Success! After hours of frantic activity, Daisy allowed herself a moment to flop down on one of the brightly-coloured sofas in the lounge and breathed a sigh of relief.

'That was brilliant,' she beamed. 'We saved people, Val. We really did it!'

'Yes, we did,' agreed Val. 'Well done, Daisy.'

'But what happens now?' Daisy suddenly wondered, sitting bolt upright as if she'd been stung by an angry bee.

'What do you mean?'

'I mean, Val, that people have *seen* us. Don't the grown ups have machines that can find aeroplanes? Radar, I think it's called? What happens when they find out where we are? Will they take you away?'

That thought filled Daisy with sudden dread.

'Do not be alarmed,' soothed Val. 'The benefits of this magic are many. One of them is that this airship does not show up on any tracking machine,' she promised. 'It is protected.'

'But people still *saw* us,' Daisy persisted. 'It will be all over the news.'

'No, it won't. Listen, Daisy. You are my new captain but you're not the first. That box has been passed from person to person over many, many years.'

'Really?' This was new information.

'Your predecessors have all been brave, just like you, and they have saved many lives, all over the world, as you did tonight.'

'I've never heard of a mysterious airship saving people in the past.'

'Exactly,' Val reassured her. 'The magic protects us. It always has. Don't ask me how it works because I cannot tell you. What I can tell you is that everyone who has ever seen this airship forgets everything almost immediately afterwards.'

'Really? That's good to hear,' said Daisy, more than a little relieved.

'Even now, those people you rescued tonight will have forgotten all about us. The police and doctors who saw us too. None of them will remember a thing. It will be very confusing for them but it's the magic's way of keeping us safe and allowing each captain to go out and help people.'

'What about pictures? People using cameras on their phones?'

'Images vanish, just the same. It has to be this way.'

'So it *is* like being a superhero. Sally was right,' said Daisy proudly. 'I don't know why I was chosen but I'm going to help as many people as I can.' She paused. 'Val, how long do I get to keep the airship? How long have the others had it?'

'Long enough,' replied Val cheerfully. 'Plenty of time to make a difference, do some good deeds and make new friends.'

'New friends?' queried Daisy.

Before she could question Val further, the airship arrived above her house. It was still dark enough for Daisy to climb down the ladder, and step off straight through her open window, which she had left wide open.

The airship dissolved back into its box within thirty seconds and it was soon sitting safely on her dressing table again.

What a fantastic night she'd had. Daisy tried to think about it but she was so tired that she simply slipped under her covers and was fast asleep before her parents came in to check on her.

With the flood over and the water level slowly falling, they watched their young daughter sleeping soundly and gave each other a warm hug, blissfully unaware that she'd just saved so many lives.

This adventure, however, was just the first of many.

Daring Daisy's courage and skill would soon be tested once again.

CHAPTER 3

Animal Magic

The weekend was looming once more and Daisy wondered if she would have a new adventure.

It had been weeks since the flood and Val had been right when she said that the box's mysterious magic would make people forget all about her heroic actions and the gigantic airship.

Not a word had been printed in the papers and she had seen nothing about it on the news, which was brilliant!

The weather was warming up nicely, as the days started to lengthen towards summer. The back garden was filled with birdsong from dawn to dusk and she often spotted a lone fox darting across her back lawn at night, on its way from one garden to the next.

Daisy loved animals and liked nothing more than to sit at her window, late at night, watching the nocturnal wildlife go about their business. With a blanket around her shoulders, she would watch until her eyelids grew too heavy to keep open.

Friday finished with the usual pile of homework to do but she never bothered with it until Sunday night, when she would rush through it quickly. Her parents were planning a night in front of the television to watch some of their favourite old movies and her two brothers would be out with their friends.

Daisy, once again, would have to keep herself occupied.

Sitting at the rickety wooden table in the back garden, sipping from a glass of orange juice, she felt the low afternoon sun warming her face and sighed.

Scanning the large garden with her binoculars, she delighted in the crisp images of birds and insects she saw. On the table, a new sketch pad awaited her best attempts to draw them.

'Can you help me please?' The voice was one she didn't recognise; soft and a little gruff.

Daisy pulled the binoculars away from her eyes and wondered who could be asking her for help in her own back garden. Strangely, there was nobody there.

'Down here,' explained the voice helpfully.

Flicking her gaze down at the grass, Daisy struggled to understand the view that awaited her. There, sitting by her feet, was a young fox.

Daisy opened her mouth to speak but nothing came out. Stunned, she closed her mouth again and shook her head as if hoping the daydream would disappear. The fox did not vanish.

'I asked you a question,' the fox said. 'You're the magical human I've heard all about, right? The one who can fly?'

'Ye..e..s, that's right,' stammered Daisy, feeling very strange that she was talking to a fox. 'But how can I understand you? You're a...a...fox.'

'Can't all humans understand animals?'

The fox paused to scratch behind one ear, trying to dislodge a hungry flea vigorously.

'Of course not. That would be silly.'

'That's odd. Animals can understand humans.'

'Well, people can't understand animals,' replied Daisy. 'Although, I can understand you perfectly well at the moment.'

'You are definitely the right human,' decided the fox happily. 'Not only can you fly but you can understand me. So the question remains,' he paused. 'Will you help me?'

Daisy hoped her parents wouldn't choose that moment to come outside and check on her. Finding their daughter talking to a fox would prove awkward to explain.

'What can I help you with?' Daisy felt very stupid even saying the words.

'Not me. I have a good friend who is in trouble. Her name is Hootie and she has a brother called Tootie. Tootie has had a terrible accident.'

'What's wrong?'

'It's very bad.'

Despite struggling to believe what was happening, Daisy pushed aside her doubts. If somebody needed her help, wasn't that why the box chose her? Perhaps it was time to have a new adventure.

'Can't you help your friend?' Daisy asked. 'Tootie, did you say?'

The fox nodded sadly. 'I can't get close enough and no other woodland creature will help, I'm afraid, so it must be you. I've been watching you for a while. I come into your garden most nights.'

'I know. I watch you from my window.'

'By the way, my name is Red. What do humans call you?'

'They call me Daisy. Pleased to meet you, Red.' Daisy was puzzled. 'So why won't other animals help this Tootie creature? I'm sure they would find it easier than I will.'

'Not really,' disagreed Red. 'Tootie is a large owl who tends to eat anything smaller than himself. We all steer clear.'

'But you said his sister; Hootie, was your friend?'

'She is. I'm a little too large for either of them to snack on so we are friends. The trouble is, I can't fly or climb trees. None of the other birds will go anywhere near an owl, especially one that's been stuck for days and will be starving hungry.'

'Can't Hootie help her brother?'

'You'd think so, yes. Sadly, they don't really get on very well. Always squabbling and arguing. Whenever Hootie tries to help, they just end up fighting with each other. Tootie yells at her to go away and Hootie gets cross and flies off.'

Daisy smiled as she realised animals and people were not so different after all. She was always arguing with her own brothers, even though they were a lot older than her. Friends at school were also always complaining about how annoying they found their brothers and sisters; taking their stuff, playing tricks on them, telling tales and so on.

'Okay,' Daisy decided. 'Of course I will help. I still don't understand how I can be talking to a fox called Red but tell me everything about Tootie and his problem.'

So Red told his story. Of how the two owls had set off to hunt one night and strayed into an area of woodland they'd never been to before.

Deciding to perch at the top of the tallest tree, on the lookout for tasty mice or young rabbits, Tootie had become tangled up in some kind of human netting. He had not seen it until it was too late; flying straight into it.

Hootie just managed to swerve out of the way in time but was unable to help her brother get free. The net was too strong, even for Hootie's razor sharp beak.

'That was three days ago,' Red finished. 'Tootie can't last much longer up there. If someone doesn't help him, he'll die.'

'Come on, Red,' said Daisy, jumping up from her chair. 'I must wait until it gets dark before I can use my airship but I promise to help.'

'Thank you so much,' Red said, wagging his furry red tail from side to side happily.

'You go and find Hootie while we're waiting for night time. Tell her that everything is going to be alright.'

'I will,' Red agreed.

'Both of you meet me back here as soon as it gets dark.'

Daisy was going to give Red a time to come back but wisely guessed that the fox wouldn't be able to tell time as humans did.

Red shot off, bolting up and over the back fence as if it didn't exist. When his red tail vanished from view, Daisy scooped up her binoculars and sketch pad before heading indoors.

Once safely up in her bedroom, she opened up her laptop and spent an hour researching everything she could about owls. Red hadn't said what kind of owl Hootie and Tootie were so Daisy learned as much as she could about the most common species.

After dinner, her parents settled down for their movie night. Darkness seemed to take forever to come but, finally, the shadows thickened and the stars flickered into view, high above her house.

The television volume was up quite loudly so Daisy was able to slip out of the back door rather than having to climb out of her bedroom window.

With the old shed ruined by the flood and a new one not yet built, Daisy had been keeping the magic box in her room again, so had carried it downstairs with her.

Laying it down on the grass, she pressed the secret button and watched as the billowing column of magical purple smoke solidified once again into her amazing airship.

Five minutes later, she was settled into the pilot's chair, talking with Val. Her first question was obvious.

'Val, do you have any idea why I was able to talk to Red today? Is that part of all *this* magic?' Daisy spread her hands wide and gestured all around her.

'When the box chose you, it did so for many different reasons. Some of them I understand and some I don't. It has always been this way. It chooses who it chooses. Some of the previous captains have been bestowed with extra abilities but I have never known a gift like yours before. Clearly, it is a magical gift so it must be from the box.'

Daisy thought hard for a moment. 'But why now? I've had the box for ages and this is the first time I have been able to talk to animals. Shouldn't I have been able to understand Rysa and Smokie? All I hear from them is barking and whining, like normal.'

'I don't have any answers for you, sorry,' explained Val, before changing the subject. 'So, what are we going to do now?'

Daisy pulled her thoughts back to the problem at hand. Tootie.

She was just about to step over to the door and peer down, looking for Red and Hootie, when there was a huge whooshing sound and something white and red suddenly flew in through the open door, landing on the floor nearby.

Daisy felt her heart leap into the back of her throat but, as the shock subsided, she realised she was actually looking at two creatures, not one.

Red picked himself up off the floor and padded towards her, whereupon he lifted a front paw and batted her softly on the knee. Behind him, remaining where she had landed, a large snowy owl regarded her through large, saucer-like eyes.

'Daisy. I would like you to meet Hootie.' The fox turned his head towards the owl. 'Hootie, this is the flying human who is going to rescue your brother.'

Hootie hopped closer and bowed stiffly, spreading one wing out in a wide, sweeping motion. 'Delighted to meet you, Daisy. Red tells me you can help my brother.'

'I'm going to try,' promised Daisy. 'If you could just tell me where your brother is stuck, we can get started right away.'

'I cannot give directions in words,' said Hootie, 'but I can fly there. You can follow me in your flying bag.'

'This is my airship,' Daisy corrected her firmly.

'My apologies,' replied Hootie. 'It just looks like a bag.'

Keen to help the trapped Tootie, Daisy told Hootie to lead the way. In a moment, the large owl was gone. Outside, she beat her impressive wings silently against the night air, hovering in one spot while Daisy started up the airship's two huge engines.

Keeping a safe distance from the spinning rotors, Hootie waited patiently as the massive airship rose gracefully into the sky and turned slowly on the spot.

Wasting no more time, the snowy owl headed off towards the west at an astonishing speed; her powerful wings and light body making her the perfect nocturnal predator.

In the pilot's seat, Daisy decided to try her hand at flying the airship herself for once. A small steering wheel on the control panel allowed her to steer left and right while a lever next to it allowed her to gain height or descend.

After a few minutes of practice, she was thoroughly enjoying herself and matching Hootie's speed perfectly.

'You make a very good captain,' Val remarked. 'I have never known any of the others to get the hang of flying so quickly.' Daisy didn't say anything but, inside, she beamed with pride.

The journey did not take long.

After less than half an hour, Daisy noticed Hootie starting to slow down until she came to a dead stop, hovering in mid-air just above the top of a very tall, majestic oak tree.

'This must be it,' Daisy said.

'I think so,' agreed Red, who had earlier decided to jump up onto her lap and perch there like a domestic cat.

'Comfy?' she laughed.

'Oh, sorry. Just gives me a better view from here,' Red explained.

'I won't be able to do anything if you're sitting on me, will I?'

Red got the message and jumped back down, stepping out of the way so Daisy could switch on the forward spotlights.

Using a small joystick, she moved the powerful beams around until she found what she was looking for.

Just below the uppermost branches, a white shape was hunched miserably, tangled tightly in what looked to be an old fishing net.

How did that get up here? They were miles from the sea, Daisy wondered. Having no possible idea, she decided not to waste time trying to find out.

Flying the airship in as close as she dared, she finally eased back on the engines, leaving them with just enough power to keep the airship hovering in one place.

'I'm going to climb down and free Tootie,' Daisy told Val and Red.

Taking a pair of sharp scissors from the kitchen drawer, she pulled open the door and watched as the rope ladder slid itself out and down. It needed no command to understand what she wanted.

'Be careful,' cautioned Red. 'It's a very long way down if you fall.'

'I'm always careful,' Daisy replied.

To prove her point, she tied herself to the rope ladder with a small safety harness before clambering outside and beginning her climb down. Red was right, she decided. Looking down at the ground far, far below, made her feel quite sick.

'Don't look down, Daisy. Just don't look,' she told herself.

Gripping onto the rope ladder tightly, she made her way down the rungs until she was finally able to step off onto a large branch, close to the trapped owl.

'Hey, Tootie,' she said with forced cheerfulness. 'My name's Daisy and I'm here to help you.'

'Nobody can help me,' whinged Tootie, clearly feeling very sorry for himself. 'Hootie has tried many times. You might as well just go away and leave me to die.'

'Don't be so silly,' scolded Daisy. 'I haven't come all this way to leave you stuck here. Just give me a minute to have a proper look at you.'

'Take all the time you want,' huffed Tootie. 'It won't make any difference. I'm doomed.'

'Silly bird,' Daisy said, keeping one eye on her footing and the other on Tootie.

Although the airship's lights were bright, she still needed a bit more to really see where to cut. Pulling a torch from her pocket, she switched it on and bathed the unfortunate creature in even more light.

A few seconds later, her worst fears were realised.

Somehow, an old piece of fishing net had been blown up into the tree and wrapped around several branches. Made from heavy cord, the net was heavy and swollen after years being exposed to rain and wind.

On closer inspection, she could see some marks where Hootie had tried to bite through it. The owl had managed to fray a few of the strands but not enough to cut right through.

'Okay, Tootie. I'm going to come closer and start cutting the net away using my scissors.'

Tootie had seen humans using scissors before so knew what they were. He knew not to be scared but he could not help it.

'Don't cut me with those,' he warned her.

'I won't. Just stay still.'

Tootie snorted angrily. 'I couldn't move even if I wanted to.'

'Sorry,' apologised Daisy. 'Now let's see what I can do.'

Moving carefully, still safely harnessed to the rope ladder, she edged closer to Tootie until she was near enough to use her scissors. The razor-sharp metal blades easily cut through the net's fibres but it still took five minutes of constant cutting before Tootie was finally free.

Daisy knew Tootie was exhausted and dehydrated, as well as being soaking wet and streaked with dirt. As the last pieces of netting fell away, his wings flapped so weakly that he would have fallen to his death if she had not been there to catch him.

'Easy, Toots. You need a little help.'

'Don't call me Toots. It's Tootie,' the owl muttered but he was secretly very relieved that this strange human girl was there to hold him tightly.

'Okay, Toots,' Daisy laughed. 'Let's get you down, shall we?'

Val knew exactly what to do and took control of the airship. Slowly she pulled away from the tree until Daisy dangled below, hanging from the rope ladder, with Tootie tucked tightly in her arms.

Moving well away from the woods, the airship slowly sank down into a nearby corn field. Within minutes, Daisy was on the ground and Tootie was standing on his own feet again, albeit still very groggy.

Before she could do anything else, Hootie suddenly zipped down from the open door and fluttered happily around her brother. Hopping up and down with relief, she checked him over and promised him a delicious meal of fresh field mouse as soon as they got home.

'Where is home?' Daisy asked her. 'Tootie needs rest. He can't fly very far at the moment.'

'Oh, it's not far away,' Hootie said. 'Thank you so much for saving my brother. If you ever need any help with anything, just let us know.'

Daisy didn't know what she could possible ever use two snowy owls for but she thanked them for the offer anyway.

Two minutes later, Tootie was beginning to get the blood flowing back through his wings again and the two owls soon launched themselves into the air and vanished into the night with a final thankyou carried back to Daisy on the breeze.

An hour later, with the airship back inside its box, Daisy gave Red a farewell stroke on his head and waved him goodbye before sneaking back indoors.

Her parents were still watching the television but the sound of gentle snoring told her that they'd both drifted off to sleep hours earlier.

Tiptoeing up the stairs, she headed into her bedroom and flopped down tiredly on her bed. A quick trip to the bathroom for a wash and to brush her teeth was all that was left for her to do.

Afterwards, snuggling beneath her soft quilt, she thought about the strange events of the past few hours and marvelled at how her life had changed since the mysterious box arrived.

She had already put it back on her dressing table and glanced over at it, still wondering where it came from and why it had chosen her.

'I am glad I was chosen,' she whispered, half to herself and half to the box. 'I wish I knew why I'm suddenly able to talk to animals. An amazing thing but very odd.'

'It's not odd. Not really,' came a very high, squeaky voice from over in a dark corner of her bedroom.

Peering intently into the darkness, Daisy could just make out a very tiny shape, floating in the air a metre above the carpet. As she watched, the shape drew closer. As it neared, it began to glow and shimmer, sparkling like a polished diamond.

As if she hadn't had enough surprises for one night, Daisy stared in amazement as a tiny flying horse fluttered over to her bed. Hovering just above her, Daisy suddenly noticed a tiny horn protruding from the centre of its head. A pink, glowing mane and matching tail complemented the white body and golden legs.

'Who are you?'

The tiny horse gave a laughing whinny. 'Hello Daisy. I'm Peggy.'

'Peggy?'

'Yes. Peggy the Pegasus.'

'With a unicorn horn too?'

'That's just where I keep my magic,' Peggy explained.

'Then do you know why I have been chosen? Do you understand about the box?'

Peggy nodded her beautiful head once. Then she flew down to land softly on the pillow beside Daisy's head.

'That is simple. The box belongs to me and I send it to very special children so they can help the world become a brighter, happier place.'

'Your box?'

'That is correct.'

'But the box is bigger than you. No offence, 'she added quickly.

'None taken.' Peggy laughed again.

'I don't understand why you chose me.'

'That is my secret to keep,' Peggy explained. 'Let's just say that I see inside every child's heart and some call out to me. The box is very old and comes from my own kingdom, far, far away.

'But the airship...and Val. How do they work?'

'That's just the magic,' Peggy explained softly. 'They are here to help you in your adventures and, at times, I may come along too,' she promised.

'And talking to animals?'

'Isn't that something your heart has always craved?'

'Yes, it is.' Daisy remembered how many times she'd watched cartoons where children were able to speak with animals and how much she had dreamed of having the same power.

'Well, now you can. You will be able to talk with any animal for as long as you have the box.'

'How long is that?'

Peggy smiled. 'There will be plenty of time for you to have some wonderful adventures, do not worry. Anyway, how about a bedtime story?'

Daisy smiled, tucked herself further under the cover, and settled down to listen.

'Oh, by the way,' Peggy added. 'Next time you see Rysa and Smokie, I think you will hear a lot more than just growls and barks.'

Daisy still had a couple more questions for her visitor.

'Peggy. You said you keep your magic in your horn?'

'That's right, Daisy.'

'What kind of magic can you do?'

Daisy had no idea what to expect by way of an answer. Thunder? Lightning? Turning people to stone? She held her breath while Peggy thought for a moment. Eventually, the tiny horse fluttered closer and winked at her.

'I can poo fairy cakes because I'm so pretty.'

Daisy burst out laughing and Peggy soon joined in. Fairy cakes? Really?

What a day she'd had...what a day indeed!

CHAPTER 4

Goblin King

The first Daisy knew of a problem was the moment the Goblin King materialised in the kitchen, just as she was making herself some cereal for breakfast. There was no fanfare or reason. Daisy simply turned around from the counter, where she had just poured milk onto her cornflakes, and started walking towards the table, only to see a squat creature waddling towards her.

Barely three feet tall, its skin was amphibian; mottled green and beige like a frog. The feet were bare and more human-like but each sported seven toes topped with long, filthy nails that curled around like the claws of a wild animal.

The face was human in size and shape, with very small ears and a large snout that was very similar in appearance to a pig. Wearing leather trousers and waistcoat, buttoned up tightly over a huge stomach, the most frightening thing about him was his teeth.

Although the mouth was human, the teeth inside his jaws were definitely not. All were sharp and pointed, in double rows, with two huge canines like the extinct sabre-toothed cat protruding over the lower lips and down halfway to his chin. They were stained and yellow yet glinted sharply.

'I will not have anyone doing magic that helps people,' the Goblin King hissed at her evilly. 'I warned them not to send the box out again. I told them what would happen if they chose a new captain for that rotten airship.'

'Who are you?' was all that came out of Daisy's mouth before the Goblin King produced a silver wand from his belt and waved it twice in her direction.

Suddenly frozen and unable to even call for help, Daisy could only watch as the bowl of cereal dropped to the floor and smashed, sending milk and cornflakes flying everywhere.

She was equally helpless as she saw her own body begin to vanish and fade away before her very eyes.

'Don't worry, little one,' hissed the Goblin King, as he too began to vanish. 'Soon we will be back in my palace, where you shall join me for...er...dinner.'

His horrible sniggering was the last sound Daisy remembered hearing and it was one that suggested she was going to be the main course of the meal rather than an invited guest!

A short while later, panic set in when Daisy's parents found the mess in the kitchen and realised that she was gone. The police were called but nobody had any clue as to her whereabouts or why she'd disappeared.

It was seeing all the police cars outside the house that drew Red into the back garden later that morning. He would not normally have dropped in to see Daisy until the evening but something felt very wrong.

He had talked to her the previous night before she went to bed. Everything had seemed fine so why would she suddenly run away?

It was while he was sitting at the back of the garden, sheltering from view beneath a couple of lavender bushes, that someone let Smokie and Rysa out into the garden. Both smelled his scent immediately and bounded over to him.

Despite their huge size and strength, Red was pleased to see them. Daisy had introduced them properly after the rescue of Tootie and they had all quickly become fast friends.

Wagging their tails and bowling him over in the excitement, Red managed to pull away from their slobbering licks long enough to ask what was going on. The dogs offered no new information.

'We didn't hear anything,' said Rysa sadly. 'My ears normally pick up the smallest sounds.'

'Me too,' agreed Smokie. 'If she'd tried to go outside or called for help, we would have heard her. She didn't.'

'I know she sometimes climbs out of her bedroom window,' said Red. 'Could she have done that?'

'No way,' growled Rysa. 'We always hear when she opens her window. She's always opening it to look at the birds or try and coax a squirrel onto the window ledge, when she isn't heading off on an adventure.'

'We heard nothing,' repeated Smokie. 'It's a mystery.'

Red explained that he had been with her for a while the night before and that she had not said anything about going somewhere.

'And the box is still by her bed,' Smokie confirmed. 'I saw it when those strange police people came upstairs to have a look around.'

'This means she hasn't taken the airship anywhere. Now I am *really* worried,' admitted Red.

There was suddenly a pink puff of smoke beneath the lavender bushes and Peggy appeared out of thin air. None of them had met her yet but they all knew who she was by the way Daisy had described her to them.

'You must be Peggy?' Red stated. 'Do you know anything about what has happened? Daisy has vanished. Nobody knows where she is.'

Peggy looked sad and a little frightened; her normally shining mane seeming dull and lifeless. She shook her head slowly but her eyes told Red that she knew something.

'If you know anything, please tell us. We have to find her.'

'I don't know for sure where she is but the fact that she's disappeared without a trace tells me that magic is involved.'

'But the box is still here! Daisy hasn't used any magic,' protested Smokie, pacing around in tight, doggy circles.

'Our magic is not the only magic in this world,' Peggy sighed. 'There are ancient powers that exist all over the world and some of them are dark and evil. I fear that Daisy has been captured by someone using dark magic.'

'Who would want to kidnap Daisy?' asked Red angrily. 'All she does is try to help people and animals. Who would want to take her?'

Peggy flew up and landed gently on Rysa's broad back. Her horn began to glow and sparkle as she concentrated as hard as she could.

Slowly the horn shone brighter and brighter until the light hurt Red's eyes if he looked directly at it.

Then, very slowly, the light dimmed and died, leaving Peggy looking more worried than ever.

'I used my magic to cast a seeking spell,' she explained, huffing and puffing from her efforts.

'Did you find Daisy?'

Peggy nodded. 'I did.'

'Where is she? Is she safe?' barked Smokie.

'She is safe for now but I fear she does not have long.'

'What do you mean?' asked Red, feeling suddenly sick and it wasn't anything to do with his breakfast of earthworms either.

'The Goblin King has her. I don't know exactly where but I do know that he has an underground palace far to the northeast, deep inside a dead volcano.'

None of them knew what a volcano was but they weren't interested in finding out. All that mattered was Daisy.

'So, we need to go there and rescue her,' decided Smokie.

The others agreed with wagging tails and threatening growls about what they would do to the Goblin King if he hurt Daisy.

'The Goblin King is a very wicked creature,' Peggy warned them. 'His magic is older than mine and perhaps even more powerful.'

'How powerful?' asked Red.

'Magical creatures of the light avoid him, and his goblin kind, as much as possible. He delights in catching and eating fairy folk whenever he can, absorbing their magic to make his own even stronger. There is nobody who can stand up to him.'

'But we have to try,' snapped Red angrily. 'I don't care how strong he is. We have to get Daisy back home.'

'I know and we will,' Peggy decided quickly. 'We'll just need help from someone who knows the island that the volcano sits on. A guide, if you will.'

'Do you know anyone like that?'

Peggy nodded slowly. 'Perhaps. Get the airship ready to go tonight. Daisy will be safe until then. I'll be back here, with our guide, as soon as it's dark. Then we can take the airship and try to rescue her.'

Time flew more quickly than they anticipated.

On one trip back indoors, Rysa successfully picked up the magic box in his jaws and sneaked it outside into the garden. Eager to get started and increasingly worried about their friend, the two dogs and their fox friend waited for Peggy to return.

As night fell, she reappeared. This time she was not alone. A very strange-looking creature appeared with her. Long and thin, with a massive rudder-like tail, it had a small head with piercing black eyes and a tiny black nose. Its fur was smooth and silky.

None of them knew what type of animal this was but a sudden explosion of fluttering above their heads immediately had the strange creature diving for cover beneath a nearby log.

'Oh never fear, Mr Otter. You are far too big to be on our menu tonight. Maybe if you were younger.'

Hootie and Tootie flew down to join the little band of worried animals, determined to be of any help they could. Tootie would never forget how Daisy had saved his life. He owed her.

Sliding out from his bolthole as gracefully as only an otter can, the stranger stood up on his hind legs and regarded them suspiciously, head tilted over to one side. His beady eyes shone in the failing light.

'Steady on. I'm here to help, not to be hassled. Blimey, if you only knew what lies ahead of us, you'd all slip back home and forget about the human. Girl's probably already been put into a pie.'

'Pie?' asked Red.

'Oh yeah, mate. The Goblin King loves fresh pie made from magic creatures, it's his favourite. Especially if he can have carrots and onions in the gravy. For a human, he might even add some peas.'

'He can't eat her!' Red was horrified. 'No way are we letting that happen. Come on everyone. Let's get the airship up and running. We have to get to her as fast as we can.'

The problem the animals faced was that none of them had fingers. The button to operate the magic airship was sunk within a recess. Daisy's fingers were perfect for sticking in and pressing it but their paws and hooves were useless. Luckily, without even having to use any of her own magic, Peggy solved the problem by using her horn to press it.

The transformation took place and very soon the rope ladder lowered down to them. The airship was too large to land in the garden, which suddenly threw up another problem.

How would they get aboard without Daisy's help?

'Anyone need a lift?' Hootie asked. 'We're very strong and can carry one of you at a time.'

'Problem solved,' Red said quickly. 'Now hurry up!'

The owls ferried everyone up to the airship cabin in a couple of minutes, at which point Val closed the door and lifted the airship high into the sky. When they reached a couple of thousand feet, with the twinkling lights of the town far below, Val asked for directions.

'Over to you,' Peggy said to the otter.

'Right. I think you're all crazy and it's a waste of time.' The otter heard the growl start in Rysa's throat and decided not to waste his breath. 'Okay, she's your friend, I get it.'

Hopping up into the pilot's seat, he started conversing with Val, giving her the directions needed.

'Who is he?' Red asked Peggy. 'He doesn't seem to want to help us. How did you even get him to come?'

Peggy snorted. 'When I need someone's help, who could resist my sweet charm?'

She showed her teeth in the equine equivalent of a smile and flicked her mane.

'Besides,' she added, 'he's the only animal I know to have been to the Goblin King's island and escaped alive. He's never told anyone how he managed it but he's quite famous for it.'

'And?' Red was sure there was more to it than Peggy's sweetness.

'I might have threatened to turn him into a fish if he didn't help,' she admitted slowly.

Smokie barked his own laugh. 'Turning him into the very thing he eats every day. Genius.'

'Not my proudest moment,' said Peggy. 'We need his help so I had to do it. I will apologise when we have Daisy safely back with us.'

'Anyway, the name's Ozzie,' interrupted the otter. 'Pleased to meet you all, even if we're all going to end up in the same pie as your friend,' he added sadly.

'Glad to know you, Ozzie,' said Red. 'I realise you don't want to be here but we can't do this without you.'

Ozzie nodded in agreement. 'Now, what can you tell us about the Goblin King's island?'

'Well, guv. Even at the speed this thing flies, we've got a couple of hours before we get there so there's some time for a tale. Settle down and I'll tell you everything I know.'

They all moved to the lounge area, leaving Val to fly the airship through the night sky. Smokie managed to open the door of the magic fridge with his teeth and they all pulled out delicious food; steak, fish, oats. Everything each of them loved to eat.

While they ate, Ozzie told them his story.

'I used to be a bit of an adventurer myself,' he began. 'Looking for treasure and excitement. It's easy enough, being an otter. I could swim to most places I wanted to go. I even swam across large stretches of sea although the salt water played havoc with my fur.'

'Go on,' urged Rysa.

'Well, one day, a mate of mine heard that the Goblin King wasn't just someone to be avoided. There was more to it. Legend says that the Goblin King is very, very old and that he's stolen gold and jewels from hundreds of unfortunate victims over the centuries. He's got a huge stash of treasure hidden somewhere in that dead mountain of his.'

'Whoever finds it will be rich,' agreed Red, intrigued. Not that animals could really do much with treasure but there were some fairies and trolls who would happily swap trinkets for food and magic wishes.

'So me and me mate; Arthur was his name, we decided to try our luck. I knew where the island was but nobody ever went there. It was too far across the sea for us to swim so we built a little raft and used our tails as paddles. We went in summer, when the sea was calm. Nice voyage actually. Peaceful.' A warmth entered Ozzie's voice as he remembered the trip.

'What happened when you got there?' asked Peggy, as enthralled by the story as the others.

'Oh, we got there, no trouble. Sweet as a nut, it was. Even made it off the beach without being spotted by the goblin guards.'

'Guards?' Hootie wondered if they might be small enough to snack on. She was feeling peckish.

'Yep. Loads of 'em. All over the island. But us otters are swift and quiet, see. We slipped right by 'em and found a trail in the woods that led us right up the outside of the volcano until it we found this huge cave.'

'Did you go inside?' wondered Red.

'Sure did, guv.' Then his tone softened sadly. 'Found out the hard way that the tunnel led straight down to the Goblin King's main chamber. Never quite got to find the loot though.'

A pause for breath added tension to the tale. Nobody wanted to hurry him but, in the end, Red urged him to carry on.

'Didn't notice a couple of guards that were hidden in a secret alcove, just outside the main chamber,' Ozzie continued. 'Spotted us and all 'ell let loose. We ran and got back to the beach but somewhere along the way they got 'old of poor Arthur. Grabbed 'im in the dark, they did.'

'Poor, poor Arthur,' said Peggy softly.

'Too right, luv. I wanted to go back but there were 'undreds of 'em chasing me by then. I jumped onto the raft and paddled for all I was worth.'

'There was nothing you could have done, Ozzie. Not against so many,' soothed Peggy. 'It's not your fault.'

'I know but it feels bad all the same. Me getting away and poor Arthur ending up in a pie. That's why going there now is crazy. There'll be just as many of 'em this time. We'll all end up on the menu tonight, mark my words.'

'No way,' argued Red. 'We have magic on our side and surprise. The Goblin King won't think that a group of animals would dare try and rescue his human prisoner.'

'We're no ordinary wildlife,' protested Smokie. 'We're a team. A crew.'

'Exactly,' agreed Rysa, nuzzling his brother's head with his own. 'The

Wilderness Crew sounds a great name for us. We won't just beat the Goblin King with magic and surprise either. There's more.'

'What else do we have?' asked Peggy in surprise.

Rysa opened his jaws, revealing his impressive German Shepherd teeth, followed by Smokie. Snapping his powerful jaws together with a ringing crunch, his eyes flashed angrily.

'We have friendship on our side and we will all fight for our friend; fight to get her back safely. I am feeling like chomping on a few goblins tonight, I'll tell you.'

'Oh I do hope they're small enough for my beak too,' agreed Hootie. Even though she had just eaten a plate of raw minced beef, she was still hungry.

So, the Wilderness Crew was born and dedicated itself to rescuing Daisy from a terrible monster.

Two hours later, as the huge airship slowly began to descend through thick clouds into a heavy rainstorm, the animals prepared to put their plan into action.

With the rain hammering on the windows of the airship's cabin and running down the glass panes in tiny streams, Val finally eased back on the engine power. Hovering a few metres above the choppy ocean surface, she manoeuvred the airship to a point about half a kilometre offshore.

With heavy clouds and no moonlight, the animals turned off the cabin lights and relied on their natural night vision to spy on the beach. Thick forest seemed to surround a single mountain, rising from the island's centre.

Unlike a normal mountain, this one seemed to be missing its peak. Instead, the mountain ended two thirds of the way up, in a circular, hollow ring.

That's just how volcanoes were, Peggy informed them.

The water was cold when they jumped in but the dogs, fox and otter had no trouble swimming quickly onto the beach. Hootie and Tootie, of course, didn't have to swim but their feathers were still well and truly soaked from the rain by the time the whole crew were back together again.

Standing on the sand, with the owls circling overhead, they all watched for any sign of goblin guards.

'If the rain stays this heavy, Hootie and Tootie won't be able to keep flying much longer,' Peggy knew. 'We have to hurry.'

The animals didn't need to discuss the plan anymore. It was simple. Get to the cave, go inside, avoid hidden guards and find Daisy. If they could do it without a fight, that would be best, but all of them were prepared to battle their way through a thousand goblins to save Daisy if they had to.

A low hoot from above told them the coast was clear. Maybe goblins didn't like the rain either?

Moving silently, they moved as one up the beach until Ozzie spotted the start of the path that he and Arthur had used on that terrible night, years before. A short while later, the animals were moving up the side of the volcano, following it closely.

Hootie and Tootie gave up watching from above when the rain came down even harder. Totally soaked, Tootie perched on Rysa's back while Hootie did the same with Smokie.

Half way up the volcano, the path ended at a cave mouth, just as Ozzie had described in his story.

Massive and dark, a human might have been frightened but the animals saw it differently. With their excellent eyes, sensitive ears and superb hearing, they could all clearly tell that the cave was empty. No sound at all could be heard except the pattering of falling raindrops.

'Come on, let's go,' commanded Red.

'We'll wait here, out of the rain to dry our feathers,' said Hootie. 'We'd be no good to you in a tunnel where we can't fly properly anyway.' She pointed one sodden wing towards a small rocky overhang next to the cave. 'By the time you come out, we should be able to fly properly again.'

The other animals agreed it was a good idea, even though it wasn't in the plan. It made sense. Without another word, Rysa and Smokie padded boldly into the cave, followed by Red and Ozzie.

Peggy sat lightly between Rysa's pointed ears, ready to use her magic horn on anything that might attack them from out of the darkness.

But nothing did.

They moved to the back of the cave, which turned into a narrow passageway that sloped gently down. With a worn, rocky floor to tread, they made good time. Before long, the sound of laughter, singing and general chaos met their ears.

They were getting close.

Suddenly, they could see hints of flickering light coming from up ahead, at the end of the tunnel. They were about to arrive at the Goblin King's lair.

Ozzie nudged Rysa in the back leg to remind him of the hidden guards but the German Shepherd needed no reminding as he loosened his powerful jaws, preparing to bite.

Peggy flew off his head just in time and Rysa sprang around a slight bend, catching two sleeping goblin guards by complete surprise. Propped up inside two little holes in the rock walls, they awoke to see a terrible monster coming at them; all teeth and snarls.

Both immediately fainted on the spot from shock.

'Good job, Rysa,' said Red. 'They'll be unconscious for hours.'

'Let's go,' Rysa ordered. 'I'm in the mood to bite a King.

Inside the main chamber, a huge party was going on. Hundreds of goblins were seated around wooden tables, drinking juice and eating piles of cakes and chocolate biscuits.

Some argued and fought while others sang and banged noisily on the table tops with their green, webbed hands.

The light in the room came from thousands of candles, stuck on the tables or placed in holders along the rock walls. It was so bright that it took a few moments for the Wilderness Crew to get used to it.

On the far side of the circular chamber, which was as large as a farmer's field, an open fire blazed. A dozen goblins were busily preparing vegetables on a chopping table while another half dozen were mixing raw pastry in a gigantic, dented copper bowl.

'We're just in time,' whispered Ozzie happily.

Despite his own fears at being back in the lair, the adventurous otter liked his new friends and really wanted to help them rescue Daisy.

'Why do you say that?' whispered Peggy.

'They haven't cooked the main course yet. Look over there.'

Peggy and Red followed the otter's pointing paw and their hearts jumped when they saw a high throne in the very centre of the chamber.

Seated on it was a large goblin, wearing a golden crown and holding a wicked-looking sword in one hand. Underneath the throne, inside a small cage, Daisy sat huddled and alone.

'Who's ready for some pie?!' yelled the Goblin King suddenly, leaping off his throne and waving the sword menacingly above his head. 'You've all had your nibbles but that's not enough, is it?'

'No! No! Pie! Pie!' chorused the other goblins enthusiastically.

'Chefs!' The Goblin King called towards the fire. 'Are you ready for the filling?'

'Yes! Bring us the human,' the cooks all called back at him. They had now rolled out the pastry to cover a giant pie dish and filled it with the vegetables and some stinking black gravy. 'Put her in and we'll finish the pie, sir.'

'Bet you wish now that you'd never heard of that box, don't you?' the Goblin King sneered nastily at Daisy.

Frightened but determined to fight them the moment the cage door opened, she glared back at him and summoned her courage.

'My friends will come for me and then you'll be sorry,' she promised.

'I'll believe that when I see it,' laughed the Goblin King. 'Now, I think it's time to start cooking.'

As the cage door lock sprung open, Daisy dived out, rolled neatly into a ball as she'd learned to do in her PE lessons at school, and was up and running towards the exit passageway as fast as her aching legs would carry her.

Behind her, she heard the Goblin King laughing as he delved into his belt and pulled out the silver wand.

Silly little human, thinking she could escape. He would simply cast another freeze spell and then she would still go into the pie.

Before he could wave his wand, however, a sudden commotion over by the entrance stopped him in his tracks.

For no reason the Goblin King could understand, dozens of his kin started screaming in terror as they tried desperately to get away from something that he could not see.

Very soon, his evil heart sank as two large dogs, a fox and an otter came crashing through the crowd towards him; biting, snapping and snarling viciously.

Terrified, the goblins fled back up the tunnel until he stood alone in his lair.

While Daisy threw herself on Smokie and Red, hugging them and getting lots of licks, Rysa moved menacingly closer.

'You stole Daisy away from us. That was a mistake,' the dog growled. 'Perhaps you should go inside your own pie?'

The Goblin King tried to lift his wand but Rysa's paw flashed out and knocked it out of his hand. It clattered noisily away and was lost somewhere under a nearby table.

'Or you could lock yourself in your own cage? That might be the safest place for you right now.'

The Goblin King shrieked, wet himself, and dived inside the cage beneath his throne. Slamming the door shut behind him, helpless without his magic wand, he slid as far to the back of the cage as he could, snivelling and wailing. He did not want to feel those teeth on his flesh.

'If you come anywhere near Daisy again,' Rysa snapped his jaws together in a bone-crunching warning, 'I will come back and tear you to pieces.'

'Can we go home now?' asked Daisy tiredly.

Yawning with a mixture of relief and happiness, the thought of getting into the airship and flying home was suddenly all she could think about.

'Home it is,' Red agreed. 'The Wilderness Crew will get you there safely.'

'Wilderness Crew?' Daisy wondered.

'We'll tell you all about it on the way back,' promised Peggy, flying in cheerful circles just above her head.

'Okay,' Daisy smiled. 'Then let's go home.'

Now she wasn't going inside a pie, she knew she'd better start thinking about what she could possibly say to her parents.

As if reading her mind, Peggy fluttered down and whispered softly in her ear. 'Don't worry. I've already cast a little spell. They won't remember a thing about it and neither will anyone else.'

'Thank you, Peggy,' Daisy sighed happily before following the Wilderness Crew back out into the passageway.

Her bed was calling her!

CHAPTER 5

Jailbreak

Daisy was feeling very pleased with herself but a little worried at the same time.

True, she *had* used her newfound magical gift to help people *and* she'd discovered a host of new animal friends who she could actually talk to. The magic box had given her the ability to communicate with animals.

Although she was delighted to be able to have had another genuine adventure, being kidnapped by the

Goblin King had cast a shadow over all the excitement.

For the first time, she realised that not all adventures ended with the good guys coming out on top.

If the Wilderness Crew hadn't found her, she would not have escaped alive. Instead, she would have been baked into a pie. It was a worrying thought.

After another week at school, which she saw as almost a welcome relief, Daisy decided that the weekend should be used to get to know her new animal friends better.

That was her plan and she was certain it would not involve flying the airship anywhere. No, she decided, she would just sneak the animals into her room at night and eat snacks with them while they chatted.

Breakfast on Saturday morning was strangely quiet. Usually her parents would rush around, making plans to go shopping or start another job in the house.

On this particular Saturday, they both sat at the dining table looking very fed up. When Daisy asked them what was going on, they pretended everything was fine.

Finishing their cereal, they then headed off to the supermarket. Both her brothers were out for the day so she was left alone with just the dogs for company.

That was when she noticed the newspaper on the table, open at the centre spread. Daisy normally avoided grown-up newspapers like the plague, preferring her own magazines or books. This time, it was the bold headline that caught her eye, drawing her in.

"Zoo to close. Animals to be relocated."

As she read it, Daisy suddenly understood why her parents had been so miserable. The local zoo was being closed, after more than fifty years. Apparently, visitor numbers were so low nowadays that the zoo could not afford to stay open. The land had been sold off to a housing developer and would soon be turned into a huge new estate of luxury homes.

'What about all those animals?' Daisy wondered aloud. She loved the zoo and so did her parents. As a family, they visited several times each year and always on Christmas Eve.

Even her brothers still came along; they loved to see all the animals too. The Christmas Eve visit had been a family tradition since her brothers were little boys, Daisy knew. They all went so often that they knew most of the animals by name.

Angrily, she finished the last few paragraphs, which explained that most of the animals had been found new homes in other zoos around the country.

'Most?' That didn't sound very promising.

The last couple of sentences sent a chill shivering up and down her spine. Any animals which could not be rehomed would have to be put to sleep by the vet, the article stated. The zoos new owners had a deadline to hand the land over to their builders and could not offer any more time.

Daisy was shocked. The article did not go into details about which animals might be at risk but there was a real sense that homes would not be found for all of them.

Daisy quickly found the number for the zoo on the internet and rang them.

The call was diverted straight to an answerphone message which explained that the zoo was now closed to visitors and thanked everyone for their support over the years. The tired, female voice on the recording sounded as sad as Daisy felt.

The rain poured down all Saturday, adding to the gloom. Daisy thought about riding her bike to the zoo but it was too far away for her to be allowed to ride there alone.

Her mum wouldn't even discuss the article with her when she returned, which told her just how upset she was. Her dad, likewise, refused to discuss it and would not take her there in the car either. He just wanted to get on with painting the inside of the garage.

Alone, in her bedroom, Daisy spent the day reading and watching her favourite music videos on the laptop.

As night fell, after another miserable meal at the table, she returned to her room to wait for her parents to go to bed. At a little after midnight, the house was finally quiet.

Slipping downstairs, Daisy opened the back door and waited for her friends to appear. They'd been looking forward to seeing her as much as she had been desperate to see them. Within minutes, the kitchen was crowded with two huge snowy owls, a fox and her two German Shepherds. A puff of fairy dust later and Peggy appeared out of thin air, flying down to perch delicately on Rysa's head, settling lightly in her favourite spot between his pointed ears.

Ozzie was missing but Daisy already knew he'd gone to visit his sick cousin. He would be away for a couple of days at least.

Daisy's original plan of having them all up in her room, for a chat and a feast, had now been replaced by a new idea. Hurriedly, she explained her problem as the animals all listened intently; the dogs actually cocking their heads to one side. Normally, she would have marvelled at how cute they looked but her heart was too full of sadness to notice.

'So the zoo is closing and the animals have to leave?' Rysa repeated. Daisy nodded. 'Why is that a problem? Lots of animals get new homes at times.'

'What *is* a zoo anyway?' wondered Hootie. 'I thought humans kept their pets in their homes, like Rysa and Smokie. Don't they?'

'Yes, for normal pets,' explained Daisy. 'Zoos don't keep normal animals.

They keep animals that come from far away.'

'What?' asked Red, bemused.

'Zoo animals come from far away places,' she repeated. 'Some of them are very large and dangerous, like lions and tigers.'

'Oh, okay.' Red had no clue what a lion was, let alone a tiger, but he decided not to look stupid in front of the others. Maybe, if he listened hard enough, one of them would explain it better.

'I've flown over that place,' said Hootie suddenly. The owl shivered and it wasn't from the rainwater running off her feathers and dripping onto the kitchen floor. 'There are some very frightening noises coming from it at night time. Roars and howls. Monsters, I think.'

'Not monsters,' argued Daisy. 'Just animals that have to be kept locked up in cages, to keep everyone safe.'

'Locked up? In cages?' Smokie grumbled with displeasure. 'How is that fair? Why bring some poor creatures away from their own homes and just lock them up?' He paused. 'I'm glad the zoo is shutting because then the animals can all go home.'

'No, they can't, don't you see?' Daisy flustered. 'When animals are put in zoos, they forget how to live in the wild. Some are even born in the zoo. They would not survive if they were put back in the wilderness.'

'That's terrible,' said Red. 'How will they find food? Do they remember how to hunt?'

Daisy spent a few more minutes explaining exactly how zoos worked. She told her animal friends how humans used zoos to educate themselves and to ensure species did not become extinct.

Eventually, begrudgingly, the Wilderness Crew seemed to understand although none of them liked the idea that locking fellow creatures up for their entire lives was somehow good for the future.

When she reached the difficult part, the animals fell silent. Not only had some of these creatures been locked up but a few would not find new homes. With no skills to survive in the wild, they would be put to sleep.

'That's awful,' decided Peggy, shedding a tiny, shimmering tear. 'We can't let any creature face such a dreadful end. We must help.'

'How do we help?' asked Tootie.

'I agree we must help,' said Red.

'We are going to help,' agreed Daisy. 'I just don't know what to do yet. That's why I wanted to talk to you all. I am open to any ideas. We have the airship and Peggy's magic but how will it help those poor zoo animals?'

'Easy,' said Tootie, fluffing up angrily. 'We take the airship to the zoo, load up any animals still left, and bring them back here to live with us.'

'Good idea,' chorused everyone else.

'I don't think so,' said Daisy. 'I wish we could do that but some of these animals wouldn't be able to live in my back garden.'

'We don't know which animals are left yet,' offered Red. 'Perhaps they are the small ones. Not the lions or tigers you spoke of before.'

Why hadn't she thought of that? She'd assumed it would be the dangerous animals left homeless but perhaps the clever fox was right.

'I think the best thing to do is go there and see what animals are left,' said Rysa, pausing to give Daisy a supportive lick on the hand.

'I agree,' stated Hootie.

'Then we can decide what to do,' added Rysa.

That was why, less than half an hour later, the shadowy shape of a gigantic airship could be seen floating silently above the dark, seemingly deserted zoo.

Most of the building's many windows were already boarded up and the open enclosures lay empty, awaiting the stinging bite of the demolition machines and earth movers.

Peering down from the open door, Daisy felt her heart sink. There was no sound at all and not the faintest glimmer of light anywhere. Were they too late?

'It seems very quiet,' remarked Red, sensing her sadness and rubbing up against her ankles reassuringly. 'That doesn't mean all the animals are gone. Maybe the ones left are just sleeping?'

Daisy felt her spirits brighten at the thought. 'Yes.' She physically shook herself into a more positive mind-set. 'Of course. It's the middle of the night. We can't give up before we've even started, can we?'

A rumble of growls, snorts and hoots agreed.

Normally, the idea of stepping inside a lion enclosure would have seemed crazy but Daisy could see that a small digging machine in one corner had already started carving out huge chunks of soil, piling it up in a heap.

If she was right, the lions were long gone.

A few minutes later, Val landed the airship inside the enclosure, which was just large enough. Torch in hand, Daisy led the way over to a metal door in the back wall, followed by the Red, Rysa and Smokie. Tootie, Hootie and Peggy flew above them.

The door was how the lions had moved in and out of their dens, she knew, having visited so often in the past. It now hung slightly ajar.

Daisy cautiously entered, wrinkling her nose against the awful stink that the majestic beasts had left behind.

The cages and dens were empty and dark, which was a huge relief. After narrowly avoiding being baked into a pie, Daisy had no plans of being eaten by a hungry lion.

Once inside the building, they moved swiftly from room to room and cage to cage. Time and time again, all they found was emptiness and silence. Even the main reception area and gift shop had been stripped bare.

It was quite spooky and she was glad she had her friends with her. She knew that Rysa and Smokie would even defend her against a lion if they had to, which made her feel a little safer.

They completed their sweep of the zoo after an hour. Daisy felt her disappointment rising with every passing minute but fought it down as she led the way into the last few rooms, out the back. These rooms were normally off limits to visitors and she strangely felt guilty as she walked past the empty offices, as though somehow it was wrong for them to be there.

Rysa and Smokie heard it first, quickly followed the Red and the owls. Blessed with very sensitive hearing and night vision, Daisy's companions were far better suited to finding things in the dark than she was.

'Stop,' growled Rysa, deep in his throat. 'Do you smell that?'

'Everything in here stinks,' said Daisy. 'How can you smell anything else?'

'My nose can smell far better than any human,' Rysa explained patiently. 'There is a background smell but it's old and fading. What I smell now is alive and new. Something is still here, I'm certain.'

'Rysa's right,' agreed Smokie, moving up alongside Daisy and thumping his tail from side to side excitedly.

'Can you tell what it is?'

'I have never smelt anything like it before, sorry.' Rysa's nose twitched madly as he sniffed the air.

Heart thumping, Daisy moved forward, past the offices, until she reached a large door at the end of the corridor. Testing the handle, it opened easily and she stepped though into a large loading area.

Used by lorries to deliver and remove animals, as well as deliveries of food and supplies, it was now empty except for a small huddle of cages against the far wall.

Flashing her torch beam ahead of her, Daisy cautiously crossed the stained concrete floor.

Hootie and Tootie were relieved to find that this room had a high ceiling so they launched themselves into the air and circled above her head;

feathers whispering to her in the darkness.

As she drew closer, the sound of movement in the cages momentarily stopped Daisy in her tracks. Gritting her teeth, she stepped closer.

After all, this was why they were here, she told herself. These animals needed help but it did not stop her feeling a little frightened.

There were five cages in all. One was large but the others were far smaller. All of them were covered with tarpaulin sheets that draped down on all sides, only showing her the bottom few centimetres of the bars.

Until they were pulled off, there was no way of seeing what was inside each one.

'What do you think is inside?' Tootie's question floated down to her ears.

'We won't know that until we have a look,' said Red, stating the obvious.

Scared as she was, Daisy got to work, very carefully pulling off the tarpaulin sheets so as not to frighten whatever might be inside the cages.

To her surprise, and disappointment, all four small cages were completely empty.

That only left the large cage, which Daisy knew must have an occupant because she'd heard movement and her companions could clearly smell something.

As she leaned closer and grasped hold of the final tarpaulin, a terrifying growl sounded from somewhere deep inside the cage.

Jumping back in alarm, Daisy felt her heart skip a beat. Simultaneously, Rysa and Smokie sprang in front of her, hackles raised, growling fiercely back at the cage.

Above her head, a bright purple glow began to shine and shimmer as Peggy prepared to cast a spell against whatever might threaten Daisy. Her tiny horn glowed and pulsed, ready for action.

'It's okay, guys,' Daisy said quickly. As her the shock subsided, she realised whatever was inside the cage had no idea they were there to help.

'We're here,' Rysa grumbled to her. 'Do not be afraid.'

'We will protect you,' agreed Smokie.

'It's probably just frightened,' Daisy told them. 'Remember why we've come. To help, not to hurt.'

The dogs immediately settled down and backed away, allowing her to approach the cage again.

This time, she thought it better to introduce herself. She cleared her throat and forced a smile onto her lips.

'Er...excuse me.' No response. 'Whoever is in the cage, my name is Daisy. I'm out here with some friends. We are all here to help you.' There was still no reply but at least there was no snarling. 'Their names are Rysa, Smokie, Peggy, Hootie, Tootie and Red.'

The cage moved slightly as its occupant shifted weight from paw to paw, unseen beneath the tarpaulin.

'Why would anyone help me?' purred a deep voice.

The voice was rich and throaty. Daisy knew immediately that they were dealing with some kind of big cat.

'It's what we do. We help anyone that needs it.'

'How are you able to understand me? You sound human. Is this some kind of trick?' The voice sounded very suspicious.

'No tricks,' Daisy promised. 'Honestly, we're here to help you.'

'Nobody can help me,' came the slow response. 'All the others have gone. My friends have all been sent away to other places. I'm the only one left but there isn't anywhere for me to go.'

'How do you know that?' Hootie asked, landing bravely on the top of the covered cage.

'I've heard the humans talking. Stan is my keeper. He's looked after me for years. He was shouting at some other humans today as my friends were taken away. I heard him saying that I needed a new home too and that it wasn't right to put me to sleep.'

'That's why we've come. To get you out,' said Daisy.

'Do I need help?' asked the voice. 'Okay, so they don't have anywhere for me to go yet so they are going to let me sleep until they do. I like sleeping.'

Daisy felt her heart sink. The creature didn't understand what it meant when humans put animals to sleep and now was not the time to explain it.

'Far better that we take you to a new home, just like your friends.'

'Why didn't they find you a new home?' Tootie fluttered down to join Hootie on top of the cage.

'I'm old,' said the voice. 'Nearly nine human years. The other animals are far younger.' A pause. 'I had an illness when I was very young too, which means I can never have cubs. It seems these new homes only wanted animals that aren't damaged.'

Fear turning to indignation, Daisy gripped the tarpaulin and whipped it off, sending Hootie and Tootie shooting up into the air.

Inside the cage, sitting upright with her black tail whipping around in agitation, the huge cat stared out at her rescuers through a pair of bright yellow eyes.

'A black panther!' exclaimed Daisy excitedly.

'That is the biggest cat I have ever seen,' barked Smokie. 'Wow!'

'And those are the largest *teeth* I've ever seen,' remarked Rysa, staring at the tips of the two huge fangs protruding from the panther's mouth.

Standing up and moving closer to the bars, the panther's whiskers started to twitch wildly as she glanced from animal to animal, finally settling her gaze on a small human female.

'My name is Shadow,' the panther sounded uncertain. 'What happens now?'

Recovering from her surprise, Daisy stepped in as close as possible but resisted the urge to put her hands through the cage bars to stroke Shadow's huge head.

'We have a flying machine. We can take you wherever you want to go.'

'Where *do* I want to go?' Shadow asked. 'Is there a new zoo that you know about? The humans said nobody wanted me.' Shadow's eyes suddenly filled with the twinkle of hope and Daisy felt terribly guilty that she wasn't able to give her better news.

'I have no idea where you can go or what home might want you, Shadow but if you come with us, I promise we will find you somewhere safe to live.'

'You can trust her, Shadow,' Rysa growled reassuringly as he stepped closer too. 'She is a very kind, brave girl. We're all her friends and we trust her. You can too.'

'We have to hurry, Shadow,' said Daisy firmly. 'I promise we will help you but we can't stay here much longer. It will start to get light soon and then the humans will come back. Are you ready to come with us?'

Shadow looked at the faces outside the bars and sensed nothing but honesty and kindness. She knew these animals and their strange human wanted to help her.

'Yes,' Shadow decided. 'Please take me with you and find me a new home.'

'Can I just check that you won't...mmm...eat any of us if we let you out?' asked Red. 'You seem very nice but I'd hate to let you out and suddenly find that your favourite food is fox.'

'Or owl,' piped up Tootie.

Daisy suddenly burst out laughing as she realised how the conversation reminded her of a very famous children's book, with a fox and owl worried about being eaten.

'All we need now is a snake,' she chuckled.

Her words made no sense at all to the animals and Red, for one, had no intention of adding a snake to the Wilderness Crew!

Rysa spotted the latches that were holding the cage door closed. There was no padlock – just a sliding metal bar. Gripping it gently in his front teeth, the large dog tugged the bar aside, allowing Shadow to push the cage door open with her head and step outside to join them.

Daisy marvelled at how sleek and beautiful she was. If Shadow was ill or old, it didn't show. Daisy could remember seeing her many times on their trips to the zoo, now that she thought back.

Despite standing next to a black panther, she was not at all worried. Shadow needed their help.

'Come on everyone, let's go.'

Finding their way back to the lion enclosure, Daisy was pleased to see the rain had stopped. The ground underfoot was still wet and slippery but it wouldn't be a problem if they were careful.

The airship still sat on the ground inside the enclosure, with the cabin door open invitingly. Quickly, they all climbed inside.

With the first pink hints of sunrise lighting up the horizon, the airship lifted high up into the sky and circled slowly for a few minutes while Daisy tried to decide where to go.

They had saved Shadow from a terrible fate but now they needed to find her a home, which was a serious problem. As an old cat, there was no way that Shadow would cope with being released into the wild. She would starve to death.

With time running out, Daisy made a snap decision. Finding the panther a new home would probably mean taking a flight somewhere far away. There was no time for that now.

'Val. Take us home,' Daisy commanded.

'Is Shadow coming home with us then?' asked Red.

'Am I?' Shadow echoed.

'Just for today,' explained Daisy. 'We need time to find her the right home. Somewhere she can be safe and happy.' Turning, she spoke directly to Shadow. 'You can stay at my house for a few hours. Then we'll find you a wonderful home.'

Shadow purred happily, which sounded very odd coming from such a menacingly cat, and licked Daisy's hand to say thank you. It scratched roughly like sandpaper but Daisy still smiled and scratched Shadow gently back behind one ear.

A short time later, as the last wisps of purple smoke poured back inside the box, Daisy and the animals found themselves back in her garden.

Daisy knew how much trouble they could be in, if they were caught. When the zoo discovered Shadow missing, they would assume the panther had escaped. They would start hunting for her. The police would be involved and, if they found her, Daisy knew what would happen to the poor creature.

But where could she put Shadow for a few hours, where nobody would discover her? In the end, the simplest answer turned out to be the right one.

The rain clouds were already starting to gather again as dawn arrived fully.

'I'm going to leave you in the back garden, Shadow. It's going to rain heavily again soon and nobody in my family will come outside in bad weather.'

'Okay,' Shadow replied, pacing around the group as gracefully as only cats can.

'But you must stay out of sight and not leave the garden, okay?' Daisy insisted. 'There will be other people out looking for you. People who won't be bothered by a bit of rain. They cannot find you. You must stay hidden until tonight when we will fly you somewhere far away.'

Shadow nodded slowly and then wrinkled her nose distastefully as a heavy drop of rain landed on its tip. Eyeing the gathering storm, the panther glanced around the garden, looking for somewhere to shelter. It needed to be big enough to hide her but Shadow could not see anything appropriate.

Peggy had an idea and flew down to hover next to Daisy.

'I could use magic to make her a shelter, if you'd like? It would be very easy.'

Daisy sighed with relief. 'Great idea. Do it.'

The tiny flying unicorn summoned her strength and channelled it through her horn. A purple flash erupted from the tip and flashed down towards the base of the oak tree. There was a brief puff of pinkish smoke, which cleared to reveal a large hole in the dirt beside the thick trunk.

'There you go,' Peggy exclaimed. 'A nice warm den under the tree, going down deeply between the roots. Just big enough to keep a panther from getting wet.'

Daisy hurried all the animals away, including Shadow, who gratefully disappeared down the hole.

Slipping in the back door and sneaking upstairs to her room, Daisy dived into bed and fell fast asleep.

She awoke a few hours later, grumpy and tired-eyed, to the sound of her parents jabbering excitedly to each other downstairs.

Guessing what it might be about, she went into the bathroom and splashed some cool water on her face before dragging a brush through her hair.

Downstairs, in the living room, her parents were watching the local news.

Surprise, surprise, Daisy thought, as she noticed the news article was all about an escaped black panther.

Luckily, the police were instructing everyone to stay indoors until the panther was recaptured. With rain still falling and everyone ordered inside, there was little chance that anyone would discover Shadow in her back garden before she'd had the chance to take her away somewhere.

The day dragged its heels, not helped by her own exhaustion. By the time dinner came, Daisy could happily have gone to bed but she had a job to do.

The question she still had no answer to was where Shadow could go? Who could possibly look after a black panther?

With darkness beginning to fall outside again, Daisy walked out into the kitchen, wracking her brains to find the answer. Grabbing a glass of orange juice from the fridge, she plonked herself down tiredly at the kitchen table and stared out through the rain-beaded window.

Before she could make up her mind about what to do next with Shadow, a quiet scratching sound at the back door caught her attention.

Puzzled, she got up from the table and walked over to the door. Opening it carefully, her heart froze when she looked down to see Red. His eyes were dark with worry and his fur was soaked through, as if he'd been waiting outside for a long time.

'What is it, Red? What's wrong?'

'It's Ozzie,' the fox said.

'What about Ozzie? Is he back from visiting his cousin?'

'Well...yes and no.'

'Which one is it?' muttered Daisy impatiently.

'He returned from his trip safely. Some of the river birds saw him this afternoon.'

'So, what's the problem?'

'A couple of swans told me that Ozzie had a visitor this afternoon, not long after he got home. It was some kind of strange bird; not from around here, who seemed to have flown a long way to see him.'

'What did the bird want with Ozzie?' Daisy had a terrible feeling she wasn't going to like what came next and she was right.

'They overheard this bird telling Ozzie that his old friend, Arthur, was still *alive*. Told him the Goblin King had been keeping him prisoner all this time. Didn't put him in a pie after all.'

'That's good news, isn't it?'

'Not for Ozzie. It seems the Goblin King gave poor old Arthur away a few days before he kidnapped you, Daisy.'

'Who did he give him to?'

'The swans didn't hear everything but they said it sounded like the Snow King.'

'Is that another goblin?'

'No, Daisy. Even the Goblin King is scared of the Snow King. Ask Peggy, she'll tell you. He's the strongest, most feared, of all the evil wizards. Legend says that he is a monstrous ogre; as big as a tree.' Red paused sadly. 'Ozzie has gone to try and rescue Arthur. He doesn't stand a chance on his own.'

'Then we have to help him.'

'We may already be too late,' Red said.

'That's why Daring Daisy and the Wilderness Crew had better get a move on. Come on, Red! Round up everyone else. I'll get the magic box.'

'What about Shadow?'

'She'll just have to come along with us for now. Besides, a set of teeth like hers might come in very handy if we run into an ogre!'

And, just like that, a dangerous new adventure was about to start...

I really hope you enjoyed sharing my stories. Keep an eye out for more!

Daisy x

Printed in Great Britain
by Amazon